THU

GOLDEN TURTLE

AND OTHER TALES

Contents

Written by Gervase Phinn
Illustrated by Linda Selby (The Golden Turtle),
Tomislav Zlatic (Amparo's Journey)
and Sholto Walker (The Naughty Leprechaun)

Collins

The Golden Turtle

Kobayashi Issei was a poor fisherman who fished the clear waters in his old leaky rowing boat near the small island of Tsunoshima, catching just enough to feed himself and his family. The other fishermen, with their large strong nets and fast new boats, would catch all the biggest and the tastiest fish. They laughed at Kobayashi Issei in his old leaky rowing boat as they sped past him for the open sea, riding the waves, sails billowing in the wind.

But the young fisherman did not mind. He smiled and waved, then cast his net and sang to himself. He loved the open sea, the taste of salt on his lips and the warmth of the sun on his face. Kobayashi Issei wanted nothing more than his small boat and a few fish each day to feed him and his family.

One day, his net sank beneath the boat. It was as if a great weight was pulling it down. Kobayashi Issei tugged and heaved, but, try as he might, he could not raise the net. All day he struggled, sweating and panting, but to no avail. As the sun began to set he tied the net to the stern of the boat and began to row with all his strength.

He had never pulled so hard on the oars. The boards creaked and the water leaked in, but he rowed and rowed. It was a slow, painful journey, but finally he pulled into the small harbour, still with the heavy weight in his net below the boat.

The other fishermen had sold their catches and they watched with interest as Kobayashi Issei struggled and strained to pull his boat up the sandy shore.

Then they laughed until they cried as the young fisherman tried to heave the net from the water, slipping and tripping and falling in the sand.

"Caught a whale, have you, Kobayashi Issei?" the fishermen mocked.

"Or sunken treasure?"

"Or a harvest of seaweed?"

"Or rocks?"

But they stopped laughing and gasped when they saw what was in the net.

It was a turtle, but no ordinary turtle. The creature's shell was a bright yellow and shone in the sunlight like plates of polished gold. Its head was huge and wrinkled and its large black eyes glinted fiercely. The fishermen ran to the shore as Kobayashi Issei pulled the huge creature up the sand.

"What a catch!" the fishermen cried.

"It must be worth a small fortune."

"Think of all the turtle soup."

"And the shell – what a price that will fetch!"

Now, Kobayashi Issei was a kind-hearted man. As he pulled away the tangle of net, the turtle stared up at him. Its eyes were no longer flashing, but looked large and sad and its beak of a mouth opened wide as it gasped for air.

Kobayashi Issei did not think twice. He turned the turtle to face the water and pushed. He pushed and pushed until the creature was very nearly at the lip of the sea.

"What are you doing?" cried the fishermen.

"He's letting it go."

"He must be mad!"

"Stop him someone!"

As the people clustered around him, Kobayashi Issei stood and faced them.

"Is this my turtle?" he asked.

"It is," they replied.

"And did I not catch it with my own hands in my own net in my own boat?"

"You did," they cried.

"And can I do what I wish with this turtle?"

"You can," they told him.

"Then I shall return it to the ocean from where it came."

With one great heave, he pushed the creature into the water and watched it dive into the depths.

"What a fool!" the fishermen cried.

"All the money he could have had for the shell."

"And enough turtle soup to eat for a year."

It was exactly a year later as Kobayashi Issei in his old leaky rowing boat watched as the fishermen sped past him for the open sea. He smiled and waved, then cast his net and sang to himself.

As the sun set and he headed for home, Kobayashi Issei heard a voice calling him.

"Taro! Taro!" it called.

The young fisherman was greatly afraid and he trembled with fear.

"Who is it who calls me?" he asked timidly.

"Taro!" came the voice again. "It is I."

Kobayashi Issei peered nervously over the side of his boat. Swimming slowly alongside was the golden-shelled turtle.

"You are a good-hearted man, Kobayashi Issei. It was you who returned me to the sea when you had caught me in your net. It was you who saved my life when others would have killed me. Come with me, Kobayashi Issei, to the kingdom beneath the sea and you will see such wonders that no man has ever seen and have such riches that no man has ever possessed. Do not be afraid, for I will take great care of you."

So Kobayashi Issei slipped over the side of his boat and, climbing onto the turtle's golden shell and clinging tightly, he sank beneath the sea and was taken deep down to the depths of the cold blue ocean. And there in a palace of crimson coral and sparkling crystal, on a carpet of silver pearls and golden amber, he saw riches beyond his wildest dreams and such wonders that no man had ever seen: gleaming sharks as big as boats, great green octopuses with arms as thick as tree trunks, giant crabs with enormous claws, lobsters the size of houses and millions of tiny silver fish like slivers of glittering glass.

"Stay here with us, Kobayashi Issei," said the turtle, "and you shall have everything you could wish for. You will never need to fish again in your old leaky boat or be laughed at by the fishermen. Stay here in the kingdom beneath the sea."

"I cannot," replied the young fisherman, "for I would long for my home and I would miss my leaky old boat. I have a wife and children waiting for me and I would be lonely here. All the riches of the ocean floor and all the wonderful sights I would see could never mean more to me than my home and family."

"Very well," said the turtle, "if that is your wish, but take with you pocketfuls of pearls and amber, corals and crystal and become the richest man in your village. For you have been kind, Kobayashi Issei, and I wish to reward you."

"I thank you," said Kobayashi Issei, "but kindness is its own reward. It costs nothing to give and is a treasure to receive. I have no need of all your riches."

The turtle swam to the surface with Kobayashi Issei clinging tightly to his golden shell and watched as the fisherman sailed for home.

And from that day to this, Kobayashi Issei's net was never empty. When the sea was rough, it swelled with fish. When the sea was calm, it bulged. In winter and summer alike Kobayashi Issei returned with the biggest and the finest catch.

When times became bleak on the small island of Tsunoshima and the sea seemed empty and the other fishermen made for home with nothing in their nets and with sad hearts, Kobayashi Issei always sailed home with a boat bursting with fish. The fishermen who had laughed at him felt ashamed, for Kobayashi Issei, a good-hearted man, shared his good fortune with all.

Amparo's Journey

Amparo lived with her four brothers, Pedro, Juan, Miguel and José, in the little village of San Colombo at the foot of the great mountains known as the Pyrenees. It was a dry and dusty village consisting of just a few white-walled houses with orange roofs and a honey-coloured church with a broken bell.

Amparo had long straight hair as black and shiny as a raven's feathers. Her eyes were dark and blue with thick lashes and her skin was a soft brown. She spent most of the day feeding the hens, watering the melons and cooking while her brothers worked on the mountain slopes trying to farm the dry and stony foothills of the Pyrenees.

Amparo might seem to the few visitors who came to San Colombo to be a very ordinary girl, but she was not. She had a terrible temper and a very stubborn streak. She was as stubborn and awkward as all the donkeys in the village put together.

One evening her brothers were very quiet.

"Well," said Amparo crossly, "I've spent all day cooking and all you do is sit there like stuffed monkeys."

"We're very worried, Amparo," said Juan quietly. "This year's crop will be very poor and we have so many bills to pay."

"If only we could ask old Uncle Carlos for help," said Miguel.

"But he lives over the mountains," said Pedro, "too far away."

"And the journey would be far too dangerous," said José.

"Nonsense," said Amparo, "I will go and see old Uncle Carlos and ask him for help."

"You can't go," said Juan.

"Yes I can," said Amparo.

"We won't let you," said Pedro.

"Oh yes you will," replied Amparo.
"I shall pack a few things immediately."

"But the way over the mountains is dangerous," said Miguel. "There are wild beasts and bandits and there is no water."

"I shall manage," said Amparo. "Now eat your food and let's hear no more about it. I shall set off tomorrow."

So the very next morning with only a leather flask of water around her waist and a little bundle of food tied in her red shawl and slung over her shoulders, Amparo set off for the village of San Fernando where old Uncle Carlos lived.

Amparo had been walking for about an hour along the dusty track over the mountains when she saw ahead a large brown cat with a short stump of a tail and long tufts of hair on its ears and cheeks. It was a mountain lynx. The creature crouched on a high rock above. As Amparo came closer the big cat snarled and spat and showed a set of sharp teeth.

"What are you making all that noise for?" asked Amparo sharply.

"Aren't you a-trembling in your shoes?" said the fierce animal.

"No," replied Amparo, "not in the slightest."

The lynx was taken aback.

"Yes you are!" it growled angrily, baring its sharp teeth. "Everybody's afraid of me!"

"Well, I'm not," said Amparo, "so if you don't mind, I've got a long journey ahead."

"I can spring three metres in the air," boasted the lynx. "I can pounce on my prey with lightning speed. I can run over snow as fast as —"

"Really, how interesting," said Amparo, "but I haven't got all day to listen to you." And with that Amparo carried on down the track, leaving the lynx with his mouth wide open in amazement.

By now the dazzling sun was overhead and Amparo felt very thirsty. Up ahead by the side of the rocky path was a large well.

"How lucky," she thought. As she was lowering the old wooden bucket down the well for some water, Amparo heard a loud and angry voice behind her.

"What are you doing?"

Amparo turned to face a very tall man with hair as white and curly as a sheep's. He was dressed in a rich red coat and carried a long black walking stick.

"What are you doing?" he thundered again.

"What does it look as if I'm doing?" replied Amparo crossly.

"Don't answer a question with a question, you bold child," snapped the man.

"Well, stop shouting at me then," replied Amparo, "you're scaring all the birds away." And she continued to lower the bucket down the well.

"This is my well!" shouted the man. "I own it! I am Don Ricardo, the richest man in the —"

"Really, how interesting," interrupted Amparo, "but I can't stop listening to you all day, I've got a long journey ahead of me."

She pulled up the bucket of water, drank a little, splashed some on her dusty face and filled her leather flask.

"You can't use my well!" shouted Don Ricardo.

"I just have," replied Amparo.

Don Ricardo was stuck for words and watched
Amparo set off again along the mountain path.

Just as the sky was getting dark and the wind became
cold, Amparo arrived at the village of San Fernando.
Old Uncle Carlos was so pleased to see Amparo that he
hugged and hugged her until she thought he would
break every bone in her body. When Amparo told him
how they needed help the old man sighed.

"I would help you if I could, Amparo, but I have nothing to give. Every month the bandits come down the mountains and take all my money. Their chief is called El Fanatico and his bloodthirsty gang steal all I have. Tomorrow is the day when they come so you must return to San Colombo before they arrive."

"Certainly not!" snapped Amparo.

"You must," said her uncle.

"I won't!" replied Amparo.

So the next day when the bandits came into the village Amparo was waiting. El Fanatico strode down the little dusty village street, a belt of bullets around his waist and a big red sombrero on his head. The other bandits all wore big black boots and carried knives in their belts and all had gold rings in their ears. They looked a fearsome sight. When they arrived at the little cottage belonging to old Uncle Carlos they found Amparo waiting at the door.

"I've been waiting for you," she said, looking El Fanatico straight in his dark eyes.

"For me?" he said.

"Yes, for you and I know why you are here."

"You do?" he said.

"Yes I do. You're here to pay back all the money you have taken from my Uncle Carlos."

"I am?" asked the bandit, amazed by the little girl's boldness.

"Yes you are." And with that Amparo pulled the fat pouch full of pesetas from the bandit's belt.

"But I'm El Fanatico, the nastiest, the cruellest, the wickedest bandit in all of Spain!"

"Really, how interesting," interrupted Amparo, "but I can't stop here listening to you all day. I've got a long journey back home. And before I go, El Fanatico, or whatever they call you, I hope my uncle has seen the last of you."

El Fanatico was stuck for words and his mouth dropped open in amazement. Nobody had ever spoken to him like that before.

Amparo's brothers were waiting for her on the rocky path into San Colombo and ran to meet her, shouting and waving. They were so pleased to see their little sister and even more delighted when she showed them the pouch full of pesetas. There was enough to pay all the bills, with some left over to buy a new bell for the church.

Amparo is now an old lady. She still lives with her four brothers in the little village of San Columbo. She feeds her hens and waters her melons and she is as bad-tempered and as stubborn as ever. One day, a famous bullfighter came to the village and . . .

Ah, but that's another story!

The Naughty Leprechaun

In the dark, wet, slippery rocks near the great castle of Oranmore there lived a leprechaun called Sean. Sean was not an ordinary leprechaun. In fact, he was very, very different from all the other fairy folk who lived thereabouts. They were all jolly, green, little elves who sang and danced, and laughed and played their fiddles until the early hours.

But Sean was round and fat and very bad-tempered. He had sharp, twisted teeth like sticks of barley sugar and big flat feet like the oars of a boat. And Sean wasn't green like the other leprechauns. He was purple. As shiny and purple as a blackcurrant. He was also very, very naughty.

Now leprechauns, as you know, are sometimes mischievous, but none was as naughty as Sean. He was horrid.

One sunny summer morning when the sea gleamed golden and a soft wind blew across Galway Bay, Sean sat in his dark, wet, slimy cave and watched four swans swim slowly towards the castle. There was a big, white mother swan and her three fluffy cygnets. As they passed Sean's cave, the naughty purple leprechaun hurled a pebble the size of a hen's egg into the water.

With a great splash it landed near the swans, which flapped their wings wildly and screeched.

"You wicked leprechaun!" hissed the mother swan. "Throwing a pebble in the water and frightening my cygnets. You might have hit one."

"It wasn't me," lied the naughty leprechaun.

"Oh yes it was," said the mother swan. "I saw you myself. Why do you do such naughty things?"

"It's nothing to do with me," said Sean, and he smiled a wicked smile.

Gathering her cygnets round her, the mother swan swam off angrily.

"You stupid old swan!" Sean shouted after her. "I hope you get swept out to sea!" Then he went back into his dark cave.

"Now, what really mischievous things can I get up to today?" thought Sean. He scratched his fat purple chin. "I know," he said, "I'll go up to the high rocks and steal some seagulls' eggs."

Sean thought it would be very funny to watch the angry seagulls screeching and screaming and circling overhead as he searched for their eggs, so the naughty leprechaun set off on his mischievous journey to the high rocks beyond the castle.

On his way along the rocky path Sean came upon a rabbit hole. He stopped and a wicked smile spread across his face.

Quickly he began to stuff pebbles and shells and seaweed and sand into the hole until it was filled right up.

"You wicked leprechaun!" came an angry voice from behind him. It was a big furry rabbit with brown eyes. "Blocking my burrow so I can't get in!"

"It wasn't me," lied the naughty leprechaun.

"Oh yes it was," said the rabbit. "I saw you myself. Why do you do such naughty things?"

"It's nothing to do with me," said Sean, as he smiled wickedly and skipped off down the rocky path.

A little further on, the naughty leprechaun came across a little mound of hazelnuts. Sean picked up the nuts one by one and threw them into the sea. Plip, plop, plip, plop they went until they were all gone.

"You wicked leprechaun!" shouted a grey squirrel with tufty ears, from a nearby tree. "Throwing all my nuts into the sea!"

"It wasn't me," lied the naughty leprechaun.

"Oh yes it was," said the squirrel. "I saw you myself. It took me two hours to collect those nuts. Why do you do such naughty things?"

"It's nothing to do with me," said Sean, as he smiled wickedly and skipped off down the rocky path.

A little further on, the naughty leprechaun came upon a little white cottage with a thatched roof. It was there that old Mrs Mullarkey lived. On her washing line were the cleanest clothes Sean had ever seen. They were blowing and billowing in the wind. The naughty leprechaun smiled wickedly again. Then he clambered over the little white fence and marched across Mrs Mullarkey's garden, crushing all her lovely flowers as he went. The washing line was tied between two big apple trees. Sean climbed up one of the trees and pulled down the line. The clean washing tumbled down onto the dirty grass.

"Hee, hee, hee!" chuckled Sean. Then he spied a bucket of milk. It was full to the brim.

He climbed down the apple tree and tipped the lovely creamy milk all over the path.

"You wicked leprechaun!" came a voice from behind him. It was old Mrs Mullarkey coming up the path. She was carrying six brown speckled eggs in a bowl. "Pulling down my washing and spilling my milk!"

"It wasn't me," lied the naughty leprechaun.

"Oh yes it was," said Mrs Mullarkey. "I saw you myself. It took me all morning to wash those clothes and milk the cow. Why do you do such naughty things?"

"It's nothing to do with me," said Sean, as he smiled wickedly and skipped off down the rocky path.

It was now getting quite late and Sean was very hungry. He decided not to go to the high rocks looking for seagulls' eggs, but set off instead across Farmer O'Flaherty's field. He knew where the farmer kept his cheese and he licked his purple lips at the thought of a nice creamy chunk. He skipped along, chuckling and singing to himself and thinking about all the mischievous things he had done, when his foot suddenly disappeared into the ground. He had stepped into a bog hole. It was a deep, slimy, smelly, squelchy bog hole and, try as he might, Sean could not get his foot out. He twisted and turned and tugged and heaved, but the more he moved the more he sank.

"Help!" cried the naughty leprechaun. "Help! I'm stuck!" He shouted again and his face turned a deeper shade of purple. Then he saw something white out of the corner of his eye. It was the white swan slowly swimming across the bay with her three cygnets.

"Help!" cried Sean. "Help! I'm stuck!"

The mother swan turned her long neck.

"Whatever's the matter?" she asked.

"I'm stuck in a bog hole!" shouted the naughty leprechaun. "And I am not here for the fun of it! Now get me out!"

"It's nothing to do with me," said the swan and swam on.

Sean twisted and turned angrily and sank a little deeper into the bog. Then he saw something brown out of the corner of his eye. It was the brown rabbit who'd just managed to clear her hole and had popped out to see what all the noise was about.

"Whatever's the matter?" she asked.

"I'm stuck in a bog hole!" shouted the naughty leprechaun. "And I am not here for the fun of it! Now get me out!"

"It's nothing to do with me," said the rabbit and her head disappeared down the burrow.

Sean twisted and turned angrily and sank a little deeper into the bog. Then he saw something grey out of the corner of his eye. It was the grey squirrel collecting more nuts from a big tree.

"Help!" cried Sean. "Help! I'm stuck!"

The squirrel looked at the leprechaun.

"Whatever's the matter?" he asked.

"I'm stuck in a bog hole!" shouted the naughty leprechaun. "And I am not here for the fun of it! Now get me out!"

"It's nothing to do with me," said the squirrel and carried on collecting nuts.

Sean twisted and turned angrily and sank a little deeper into the bog. He was now up to his chest in the deep, slimy, smelly, squelchy bog. Big tears rolled down his shiny purple cheeks.

"Nobody will help me!" he whimpered. "I'll sink in the bog without a trace." Then he saw something red out of the corner of his eye. It was old Mrs Mullarkey in her new red shawl coming down the rocky path.

"Help!" cried Sean. "Please help me, I'm stuck!"

Mrs Mullarkey stopped. "Oh, it's you, is it?" she said. "That naughty purple leprechaun. The one who crushed my flowers and dirtied my washing and spilt my milk!"

"Yes," whimpered Sean, "and I'm stuck in a bog hole and I'm sinking. Please get me out."

"Well, if I do, I want you to promise never to get up to your mischievous ways again."

"I promise, I promise," said Sean.

"Very well," said Mrs Mullarkey, "it just so happens I have my broken washing line in my basket. I was taking it round to Farmer O'Flaherty's to be mended. Tie it round your waist and I'll pull you out."

Sean tied the line round him and old Mrs Mullarkey heaved and hauled and tugged and pulled, but the leprechaun didn't move.

"Can somebody help me?" shouted old Mrs Mullarkey.

The rabbit hurried from her hole, the squirrel scurried over from the tree and the swan flew from the bay to help. They heaved and hauled and pulled and tugged and soon Sean was out of the bog. The swan and the rabbit and the squirrel and old Mrs Mullarkey all smiled. For Sean looked very funny all slimy and muddy and dripping wet.

"I hope you've learnt your lesson," said
Mrs Mullarkey.

"I have," said Sean.

And from then on he was the most helpful and
happy leprechaun on the Oranmore coast.

WANTED!

LEPRECHAUN

Goes by the name of Sean

description:
round and fat
sharp, twisted teeth
big flat feet
purple all over

character:
bad-tempered
naughty
tells lies
spiteful

last seen wearing:
red and yellow check trousers
red waistcoat
yellow scarf
brown hat

WANTED FOR

- hurling a pebble at the swan and her cygnets.
- planning to steal some seagulls' eggs.
- blocking up the rabbit's burrow.
- throwing the squirrel's hazelnuts into the sea.
- trampling over Mrs Mullarkey's garden.
- pulling down Mrs Mullarkey's washing line.
- tipping creamy milk over Mrs Mullarkey's path.

BEWARE

IF FOUND, DO NOT HELP THIS LEPRECHAUN,
EVEN IF HE GETS STUCK IN THE BOG, UNTIL HE PROMISES TO
MEND HIS WAYS.
IF HE DOESN'T PROMISE, CALL THE
FAIRY FOLK FORCE ON 123456.

❀ Ideas for guided reading ❀

Learning objectives: compare different types of narrative texts (traditional stories and folk tales) and identify how they are structured; explore how writers use language for comic and dramatic effects; tell a story using notes designed to cue techniques such as repetition, recap and humour

Curriculum links: Geography: Passport to the world; Citizenship: Choices, Living in a diverse world

Interest words: folk tale, Oranmore, leprechaun, mischievous, billowing, whimpered

Resources: picture of a leprechaun, large whiteboard or screen

Getting started

This book can be read over two or more guided reading sessions.

- Read the title and blurb on the front and back covers. Discuss what may happen in folk tales, and whether they are likely to be fact or fiction. Ask the children what other folk tales they have read.

- Focus on the third tale: *The Naughty Leprechaun.* Show a picture of a conventional leprechaun. Ask children what they know about leprechauns and where they come from.

- Read the first part of the story and the description of Sean. Pause at the end of p36 and ask children to predict the naughty things that Sean will do to the rabbit hole, and what may happen to him in the end.

Reading and responding

- Model reading the rabbit incident aloud, using different voices and strong expression. Were the children's predictions right? Ask children to read the story aloud as a group to p41.

- As a group, recount the events so far, introducing some of the repeated language ("'It wasn't me,' lied the naughty leprechaun").

- Note the features that help to make this a folk tale (repetition of events, repetition of language, animals who talk).

- Ask children to continue reading to the end of the story.